Legal Notes

Unique Creations Publications © 2019

What Makes You Unique:

Reaching for your goals no matter who doubts you is what makes you unique. Not letting this world take your creativity and remaining humble no matter what causes you to stand out. When life gets tough, don't give up, just keep pushing for the stars. The people that shine the brightest are often the ones who have been down the darkest roads.

Dedication

This book is dedicated to my mother,

Doris Perkins,

one of my main supporters.

Thank you for believing in me even

when I didn't believe in myself.

Acknowledgments:

I would like to give a special thanks to all the Curvy women around the world who have self-love, confidence, and self-esteem. We are here to stay whether people like it or not. Our curves don't hurt anybody; if anything, it motivates us to be a better person than the ones who degrade us, staying strong through it all and never letting this world break us.

Synopsis:

Ocean Ray is a country girl at heart but has no choice but to embrace the city life after losing her father. Moving to New York to live with her auntie was her mother's best option for herself and her children until her mother passed away from cancer.

Now that Ocean has learned the city, she is making new friends. Not being used to befriending people outside of her race, she will soon learn that a person's color doesn't determine their values.

Even after several traumatizing experiences, Ocean finds herself falling for the one person who will never understand her struggle in life but will still always find a way to be there for her. Nick Rizzo is a New York native Italian with a heart of gold. He's struggling with his own problems, one being he never imagined-falling for a woman of Ocean's size or color. Will Ocean be the woman of Nick's dreams, or will he let her color and size get in the way?

When things get shaken up, these two will have no choice but to be there for one another in the end. With them both coming from two different backgrounds, they will see just how much they have incoming and that they're not so different after all.

Battling Mental health and Logic, Ocean tries her best to stay afloat. Will logic and reason turn the growing relationship into dust, or will it bring these two closer together?

Can true love really be ignored, even when the bar-

riers of color, financial status, and family try to stand in the way? If true love conquers all, shouldn't Nick and Ocean be together?

Chapter 1

NICK- THE MEETING

eing a lawyer in the big apple had its ups and downs. Yeah, the money was good, but you had to be in contact with some of the ruthless gang bangers to get to that real paper. Pulling up to Big-Mike's crib, was a bit scary for me. Big-Mike was the leader of the blood gang which was well know in Bedford-Stuyvesant area, which was only one of the many ghetto hoods located in New York. I had most people called it Bed Stuy for short. Bed Stuy was one place that no white or Italian guy could just pull up to without answering for it so of course the shit had me nervous. I could see all of the blood gang members standing outside of Big-Mike's house. The Blood gang memebers would always wear red flags around their heads or some where onto their body that was notica- ble to represent their set. The red flag just let every- one know who they were rolling with, and most people around Brooklyn were scared of them. I knew what everyone said about them, how they wasn't to be fooled up with but right now, the only that was on my mind was getting paid.

"Wuz up, man? Who you lookin' for, son?" one of

the gang members at the door asked me.

"I'm Rick Rizzo, Big-Mike's lawyer, and we have a meeting today. Can you let him know that I'm here, please?" I replied as nicely as I could. I hated this part of my job because I always imaged how shit would go down if things didn't go the right way.

"Hold on, son," he said as he walked inside the house to see if Mike wanted to see me or not.

He stepped back out the house peeking his head out of the door as he was waving his hand at me, gesturing for me to come on inside the house. I was nervous, and the palms of my hands were sweating as I tried my best to hold on to my briefcase with all of my paperwork inside of it. As I was making my way inside of the townhouse, being escorted by the gang member who stuck his head out of the door, I made my way to the back to meet with Big-Mike. My heart pounded at over a hundred miles per hour but I tried my best to stay clam. Finally, he stopped right in front of me looking back at me with this look on his face that kind of scared the shit out of me.

"My man's in there, son," he said as he walked back down the hallway heading towards the way that we came inside the house.

"Thanks," I said as I just stood at the door, fixed my tie and gave myself a talk. You need this money, so pull it together.

That's when I pushed the door open, and there sat Big-Mike standing six-feet-seven with big muscles and tattoos all over his body with his red flag tied around his head.

Uniquely Lashay

"'Bout time you showed up," Big-Mike said.

"I got the paperwork. All you have to do is sign it and give me the percentage of the money we agreed on," I replied.

"I know how this shit works, my nigga. Have a seat because I need to go over a few things that you might not understand," Big-Mike said in his deep voice.

"Alright, well, let me take a seat so I can write this all down," I replied as I took a seat in front of his office desk. Before I could sit down good, Big Mike started giving me the rundown.

"Listen, my man, Killa Joe is facing a lot of time because not only did they catch him with five kilos of cocaine, but this nigga also shot and killed two of the cops that busted him. Do you think you still can get him off?" Big Mike asked.

"Look, I'm being honest. I can get him off the cocaine charges, but he might still have to do a few years for killing the cops. It's no way the judge is just going to let him off Scott-free with them murders, but as I say always, I will try my best," I announced, unsure if I could even beat the murder charges at all. I sat there thinking, What the fuck is you gettin' yourself into?

"Here is the money," Big Mike said as he tossed a big black bag into my lap.

I unzipped the bag and looked inside just to find it filled with money. It was the thirty-thousand dollars I told him I needed up front.

"You can count it if you need to."

"I'm good. I trust you," I replied because he had never fucked me over before. I had planned on letting the bank teller count it as soon as I made it to my bank. They had a money counting machine which made shit much easier for me than trying to count it by hand.

I grabbed the bag of money and said, "Ok, I'm about to go get started on this case. I will call you once there is an update on the case."

"I trust that you gon' do your best for my friend, right?"

"I promise you I will do everything that is in my power," I replied as I walked out the room with the bag on my right shoulder.

Leaving out the townhouse, I got this bad vibe, but I just shook it off. I could feel all the gangsters standing outside of Mike's place staring at me, but I just looked down trying not to make eye contact.

❦

Once I got into my Ferrari, I pulled away as fast as I could. Making my way to my bank to drop off this money, my cell started ringing off the hook. I glanced down at the phone to see who it was blowing my phone up, and it was my best friend, Da'wan Washington. I hit the Bluetooth on my car so I could still talk and drive at the same time. I loved that about my Ferrari.

"Hi man, what you up to this weekend?" Da'wan said as soon as he heard me pick up the phone.

"Nothing, didn't you have court today?" He was supposed to be working on this big case, so I just knew he would be in court all day.

"Man, you know me. I put in that work and had the judge throw out my guy's whole case. They didn't have enough evidence to make the charges stick," Da'wan announced.

"Your ass is good. I might need you to look over this new case I just took whenever I do pull up on you," I replied because I was gonna need all the help that I could get with everything Big-Mike was telling me this case had going on.

"You know how it goes, but I do my best for my clients. Sure, I don't mind looking it over for you, just bring it to the house when you pull up this weekend," Da'wan replied.

"Saturday night, right? What time should I pull up?"

"Eight o'clock, and man, don't be late. Mercedes is bringing her friend, and I hoped you two could hit it off. She's single, and you're single, so you guys can mingle a little," Da'wan replied.

"I'll be there, and Da'wan, she better be cute," I said before he could hang up the phone.

Da'wan was my homie, but his ass loved to party, and since he got this new crib, he was having a house party. See, me and Da'wan met at Harvard University when we were both undergraduates trying to make it through college which was one of the hardest things I had ever done, so Da'wan and I started kicking it and helping each other with homework and big projects, and we had been tight ever since. They say unless you

struggle or go through a hard time with a person, you will never know them truly. I felt like us pushing each other to do better why we was in college showed me a lot about him. Da'wan was one person in this world that I knew I could trust.

I had to go by my mother's house and check up on her. I was really surprised that she hadn't called me all day. My mother was a white lady with dark brown hair, hazel brown eyes, and she was on the curvy side. I was still shocked that she married an Italian man like my father. To me, my mother could have done so much better than my old man. Once I dropped off this money, that would be my next stop--my mother's house.

Once the money was dropped off and I knew exactly how much it was, I was satisfied. Big Mike gave me exactly what I had asked him for, so now my bank account was looking swole as fuck. Pulling up to my mother's three-story house reminded me of the old days when I was little. My mother used to make cookies for me and my friends whenever they would come over to visit.

I got out my car after I parked it right in the driveway next to my mother's dark all grey BMW 2019. Yeah, my mother had a little money herself because she was a lawyer just like her son. My mother stepped out onto her porch as soon as she heard my car pull up outside like she always did, not even giving me a chance to enter the house to see her. "My handsome son," my mother said as she placed a small kiss onto my right cheek.

"Hi, Mother. I missed you," I replied as she moved my head side to side to place a kiss on each cheek.

Uniquely Lashay

"Where have you been?" my mother asked.

"I went to see my old man, then I made a stop at the bank, and now I'm here with you," I replied.

"How is your father?" my mother asked in a nonchalant type of way.

She really didn't give two shits about my old man, but she kept it bland only for my sake.

"You know he keeps on bring up this arranged marriage," I told my mother waiting for her input on the situation.

"You don't have to do anything you don't want to do. I told you a long time ago to keep making your own money, and there was nothing Nichols could do to you besides get mad, son," my mother uttered. She was right though; it was my life, and it should be my choice who I end up with.

❧❧❧

Chapter 2

OCEAN- THE PARTY

Next weekend had rolled around before I knew it, and I couldn't believe that I had let Mercedes talk me into coming to this house warming party her boyfriend, Da'wan, was having tonight. I had picked out my all black bodycon Versace dress, and I couldn't lie, I just loved the way it highlighted all my curves. The black and silver color scheme made my toffee color skin radiate even inside of Da'wan's dimly lit living room. Mercedes wasn't looking to bad herself. She had on a red Versace bodycon dress with her back out that had a gold and red color scheme that made her gold tipped dreads glisten from across the room. We both stood up at the bar that was placed in the inside of the living room in the back corner ready to order us a drink. "What are you drinking on tonight?" Mercedes asked me as she looked into my direction.

"I'll have the usual," I replied, not having to tell her exactly what I wanted.

"D'usse on the rocks," Mercedes said, looking at me as she placed my order. That was my bestie, so I knew she would know exactly what I wanted without my in-

put.

D'usse was a new cognac liquor that the rapper Jay Z had put out, and everyone in New York was fucking with it. I had tried it a few months back, and I loved how smooth it was. I had been drinking it ever since. Mercedes, on the other hand, was a vodka type of girl, so Ciroc was her go-to brand. I loved Mercedes, but I couldn't drink white liquor.

"You know Da'wan homeboy is coming here tonight to see you?" Mercedes announced as she handed me the cup of D'usse.

"Girl, I have told you I'm only here to have a good time and spend time with my best friend."

"Can you please just be nice for me?" Mercedes asked as she gave me this puppy dog look.

"Ok, sure, I will meet him, but I'm telling you he better be cute," I said, warning her about last time.

"He is cute, just chill," Mercedes said as she took another sip of her Ciroc on the rocks, frowning up her face as she swallowed her sip of drink which let me know that it didn't taste that pleasant.

Before we could say another word, Da'wan walked up to us. "Hi ladies, I'm happy you two could make it," Da'wan said.

"Hi boo," Mercedes uttered as she leaned over to place a kiss upon Da'wan lips.

"How are you doing tonight, Da'wan?" I said as I waved my hand just in case he couldn't hear me because the music was so loud.

"I'm good actually. Did Mercedes tell you about my

man Nick wanting to meet you?"

"Yeah, she was telling me a little about it." I smirked.

"Why are you doing all of that?" Da'wan asked.

"She doesn't think he will be cute, but I told her to just chill," Mercedes said as she hung her arm across Da'wan's shoulder.

"I ain't gay or nothin', but my man look decent, for real," Da'wan said, reassuring me that the dude Nick wasn't ugly.

"Ok, I should just take your word for it, huh?"

"He should be pulling up any minute now," Da'wan announced as he looked down at his watch. Looking up from his watch, he looked around as I saw a white guy with dark brown hair entering the front door of his new Condo.

"There he goes right there." Da'wan pointed as he made his way towards the guy leaving us still over by the bar.

I tapped Mercedes on her shoulder trying to get her attention. "That's him," I said.

"That's who?" Mercedes asked.

"The guy that grabbed me by my waist that almost knocked me down last week," I said, trying to make her remember the accident I had told her about.

"Who? Nick, Da'wan's friend is the white guy that almost knocked you down?" Mercedes asked trying to gain clarity of what I had just told her.

"Yes, that is exactly what I'm saying."

"So, why were you mad again? He is fine as hell, Ocean," Mercedes replied as she giggled a little.

"Mercedes, this is not funny. What if he remembers me?"

"I'm sure he won't, just be nice," Mercedes said. I could see Da'wan and Nick making their way over to where we were beside the bar.

"Ladies, this is my homie from Harvard, Nick Rizzo."

"Hi Nick, we have heard so much about you. This is my best friend, Ocean," Mercedes introduced us as she shook his hand.

"Hi, I'm Ocean," I mumbled, praying that he wouldn't notice who I was.

"Ocean, that's a pretty name. You look so familiar to me, have I seen you before?" Nick asked as he shook my hand.

"I don't know, New York City isn't that big," I said, not really answering his question at all.

⁂

Nick had on an all-white Armani suit with a white shirt to go on the inside of it, and he had on some black Armani shoes that matched. I couldn't lie, he was clean as fuck and looked just like a gentleman. Too bad he wasn't my type because I had told Mercedes over and over again I wasn't into white guys or Italian guys. Before I could turn to Mercedes and give her that look,

Mercedes and Da'wan had already walked away giving me no choice but to talk to Nick.

"So Nick, what is a white guy dressed as nice as you doing hanging out with someone like Da'wan?" I asked him, waiting on his answer.

"Da'wan and I met in college. Harvard wasn't easy, so we became friends and have been friends ever since," Nick said, giving me the perfect answer.

"Wow, I would have never known that, but I see you two have more history than I thought."

"Oh, you didn't think I just was the type who hung around black people just to seem cool, did you?" Nick looked at me and asked.

"I was just asking, but I don't know what I think to be honest. Where I'm originally from in Georgia, I never even got a chance to ask white people nothing, so since I been livin' here in New York, things are much different for me," I replied without giving a thought about what he would think about me.

"Well, I don't see color when I see people. If a person treats me good, I just try to treat them better," Nick replied again with another perfect answer.

"I hear what you're saying, but let's just be honest here. Not seeing color is something we all want to believe, but how the police are killing young black men makes it hard to overlook anybody's color."

"Now I know where I saw you before. You'er the girl I ran into on the sidewalk. Yep, that's you. You were mean as hell to me that day," Nick said.

"Yeah, I'm not gonna lie, that was me, and I wasn't

mean to you. You were the one not looking where you were going and nearly knocked me over, not to mention you made me drop my purse," I replied, giving him a look that only a mother gave to her child when he or she had done something wrong.

"You right, my bad, and I didn't mean nothing by what I said at the end either. You know, the part about you not being my type," Nick said trying to clear up his meaning.

"Look we just talking it's not like nothing is gonna come of it besides you didn't hurt my feelings it will take a lot more to make me feel bad about my self," I announced.

Just when I finished my sentence Mercedes and Da'wan walked back up and I could tell that Mercedes ass was a little tipsy.

"Nick you over here being nice to my homegirl ain't you," Mercedes utter as she walked up.

"I like to think I am," Nick uttered.

"Come on man, I wanted to look over the paperwork for your big case before I get too tipsy," Da'wan said pulling Nick away to walk with him.

Has Nick and Da'wan walked off Mercedes whispered in my ear? "So what do you think about Nick?"

"Mercedes if you weren't my best friend I would have been hurt you. I done told you I want a black man, not a white nor an Italian one," I said in my serious tone.

⤬

Chapter 3

NICK- CELEBRATION

It had been a month since I had seen Ocean at the house party, and I still couldn't get this black thick beauty off of my mind. I was happy that everything with the case I took for Big Mike was going good. I had gotten Killa Joe visitation rights so now he was able to see his family and friends. Other than how Ocean had treated me at Da'wan's house party, my life seemed like it was falling into place. My father had texted me yesterday and told me to make sure I came by the house of one of Italian's biggest celebrations they would have for this year. It was known as the Italian Independence Day which was always on March 17th, but we would be celebrating it on the Saturday after instead. I was excited to get to see some of my family members I hadn't seen in a long time.

Getting up out of my bed, I sat up on the side of it when my cell rang. I leaned over the bedside table to see my mother's picture come across the screen. I hurried up and picked up the phone with morning breath

and all. You guys know that morning breath that you could smell yourself as soon as you opened your mouth.

"*Morning Nick,*" my mother said soon as I answered the phone.

"*Good morning, Mother,*" I said after I took a deep breath.

"*Why are you breathing so hard? What's wrong, son?*" My mother knew me so well and could always read me like a book so she could tell when something was wrong with me.

"*It's nothing, Mother. I'm fine,*" I said, trying to convince her that everything was peaches and cream.

"*No, you're not, Nick. Tell your mother what is bothering you.*"

"*It's just I met this girl, and she is really cool, but I don't think she likes me at all. I know it's crazy because the ladies normally are going crazy over me, but not her. My thing is I don't think she likes me because I'm a white Italian guy,*" I replied, waiting for my mother's reply. My mother started to giggle after I said what I had to say, now I was feeling really stupid.

"*Son, your story sounds like your father and me when I first met him. He was head over heels for me, and I was too busy with school to even notice him. That didn't stop your father for coming after me, and he was very persistent in dating me. Even when I ignored him, he would do things that made me notice him. He went so far as, him even finding out my favorite ice cream. How I still don't know still till this day how he pulled that one off. If she is as special as you say she is, then go the whole nine yards to make sure she knows how special she*

is to you," my mother uttered.

Her words vibrated through my ear as I listened to her, and I knew she was right. Maybe I hadn't put enough effort into trying to make Ocean like me beyond my skin color.

"*You're right, Mother. I love you and will call you back later,*" I replied.

"*I love you too, Nick,*" my mother replied then hung up the phone.

After I hung up the phone with my mother, I shot Da'wan a text message.

Me: What is Mercedes' phone number?

Da'wan: 917-333-2002

Me: Thanks, I need to ask her something about Ocean.

Da'wan: I knew you had a thing for her.

Me: Bye, man.

I got up and found me an all-black Armani suit with a black shirt to go in the inside of it and a pair of my Armani white shoes to go with it. Then I pulled out my all-black Gucci shades which matched my outfit perfectly. I planned to be fresh as fuck walking into my father's family celebration this afternoon. Once I had all my clothes laid out on the bed, I grabbed me a towel out of the towel closet in my room and made my way to the bathroom to take me a much needed shower. I turned on the water so the water could get warm first, and once it was warm enough, I stepped into the step in shower in my bathroom to take me a shower. As the warm water pierced my body I felt all the tension I had built up about Ocean go away. I just didn't get

Uniquely Lashay

Ocean, she was a successful and beautiful black woman to me. It seemed she just didn't want to give me a chance because I wasn't a black guy. How I see it, if a man loves you as his woman, color shouldn't matter as long as he's treating her like the queen she carries herself as. Once I finished a good thirty-minute shower, I got out and put the towel around me, that's when I heard my cell chirp again. I rushed out of the bathroom to make it to my phone, and that's when I saw the text from my father that I didn't want to ever see.

Father: Bella will be at the house this afternoon, so please be on time.

I read the text and decided not to text him back. The thought of seeing Bella again made me feel some type of way. You ever had this puppy love with someone then all a sudden you never see them again? Well, this was where I was at with this situation. I remember playing with Bella as a kid when our parents made the arrangement, but after that, she moved away. It had been almost ten years since I saw her, but I was nervous like it was my first.

I finished getting dressed and stood in my body mirror for a minute that sat in my room. I was looking like a white Denzel Washington with my all-black suit on and my black Gucci shades. I was ready to turn heads and have all the ladies at the party watching me.

I jumped into my Ferrari and headed to my Pops' house. I knew everyone and their mothers were gonna be there because that's just how my old man was. He liked to do it big whenever he did have anything at his house. It wouldn't surprise me if he didn't have the Mayor of New York there standing in his backyard

right beside him. I loved my pops, but he could be a tad bit extra when he was giving a party of any kind.

After I pulled up to his gate and pushed in the digits to get in the gate, I took a deep breath because I knew I was about to walk into the heated pit. As soon as I got out the car, I was approached by my father. He gave me a hug and a kiss on the cheek. "Sei in ritardo," my father said which meant "You are late," in Italian.

"*Conosco mio padre,*" I replied which meant "I know, father," in Italian.

As we made our way to back of the house where everyone else was, I noticed Bella and some of her friends standing across the way. I could spot her anywhere. She stood five-foot-seven-inches with dark brown hair and dark brown eyes to match. Her hair and eye color were still the same since I last saw her when were only seven years old. She had this mesmerizing look about her, and she was a sight to see. She had a small frame but a nice shape to go with it. As soon as her eyes locked with mines I knew she had spotted me as well. That's when my Pops put his right hand up on my shoulder and gave me a look like he was saying you better be nice. Before I could give him the look I wanted to give him back, Bella ran up to me and grabbed me by my arm. "Nick, wow, you have gotten so big," she said in her cute soft voice.

"Bella, is that you?" I asked, playing it off like I really didn't see her.

"Yeah, it's me. The grown up version of me any ways," she announced. That's when her friends made their way over to us, and I could hear them whispering

about me like I wasn't standing there.

"Is this Bella's husband to be?" girl number one asked girl number two.

"That's him, M. Man of the hour," girl number two replied.

That's when Bella gave them both a nudge with her elbow. "Would you two hush? You guys are embarrasing me."

"Nice to meet you all too, ladies," I said.

They both started blushing and whispering even lower so Bella nor I could hear them.

"You look nice," Bella said, giving me a push.

"I see you still don't know how to keep your hands to yourself," I replied and shoved her back a little.

"I'll leave you two love birds alone," my father said as he walked away.

"Love birds." Bella repeated.

"He be goin' too far with this marriage arrangement thing our parents put together," I replied.

"Oh, that's what his whole deals been today. He asked me had I seen you since you were older earlier," Bella replied.

"Yeah, I don't even think I'm ready for marriage, let alone a wife," I announced, giggling after saying that.

"I understand, trust me. That arrangement is all my parents talked about for years. I'm like you, I'm just trying to live my life. I don't think I'm ready to be

married let alone a wife," Bella said like she was cer-
tain and had a made up her mind.

Chapter 4

OCEAN- THE NAIL SALON

I hadn't heard from Mercedes in about a month now. Her and Da'wan had pissed me off trying to play matchmaker instead of letting me find my own Mr. Prince Charming. I knew I was twenty-six years old without a partner but them trying to focus me to talk to someone wasn't going to make it happen any faster. The guy Nick was nice and all but I wasn't feeling him. I still had a lot on my mind with me starting to do these singing shows for the night club down the road from my Aunty Netty's apartments. I thought getting back into music would be a good thing for me so that's just what I planned on doing. Not just for my sakes but for my Pa. He knew I loved music, and I felt like getting closer to music would help me heal the big whole I had in my heart that just couldn't' be filled by anyone.

I was sitting at the house on this fine Saturday and of course, I had nothing to do. That's when I heard a

knock which sounded just like Mercedes little signature knock she always did. You ever had someone knock on your door and you could just tell by the knock it was them, well that how it was for me with my best friend. Even though, I was mad at her I knew I couldn't stay mad at her long. She would always come back around to check up on me like she always had ever since I was just a little girl.

I jumped up and nearly ran to the door because I knew exactly who it was. Soon as I opened the door Mercedes sprung into my aunty's apartment without even saying, hi like she always did.

"What are you doing here," I asked her before she could ask me about food like she was known to do.

"Look, I and Da'wan are sorry. We didn't mean to be so pushy trying to hook you up on a blind date and all," Mercedes said admitting she was wrong. I was shocked to be honest because that was a first. She had never admitted to me when she did wrong so I knew from just that gesture that she was being genuine.

"It's cool, I know you just want me to be happy. I really am trying it's just I have some much other stuff on my mind like starting my music career," I replied.

"Well, I actually come to take you to get your nails and toes did if you're up to it. It's all on me and my way of apologizing for being so pushy," Mercedes uttered.

"I don't have anything planned so I guess you came at the perfect time," I said.

"Ok, grab your jacket and make sure you are warm because it is still snowing like crazy," Mercedes an-

nounced.

Which I figured it would be snowing like it always is in New York around winter time. I grabbed everything that I need to keep me warm from my scarf to my hoodie. I didn't like New York's cold weather at all and after all these years I wasn't used to it. Just as we were walking out of the apartment door to head to the cab, my Aunty Netty was getting ready to walk in.

"Where are you two hot mama's headed to," aunt Netty asked?

I was actually happy to see my aunty because when I woke up this morning she had already headed out so I didn't know where she was. I called her cell like two times but it kept going to the voicemail which I knew that it would because my Aunty Netty don't know how to really work her cell phone yet. Although, she had one she barely used it.

I rush up to her as I gave her a big hug and a kiss on her cheek then said, "We headed to the nail salon Aunty Netty. You want to tag alone," I asked?

"Child, no it's cold out here and besides I am, beat from working all morning. I'm about to head inside to get me some rest," she said.

"Good to see you, Aunty, Netty," Mercedes said before getting into the cab after me.

"Aunty Netty? That is not your Aunty Mercedes," I announced feeling some type of way about her claiming my aunty.

"Why can't she be my aunty too? I have been coming over to her house for as long as I can remember to visit you and after all these years she is my Aunty

Netty too," Mercedes said tooting her nose up at me.

"Ok dang, she can be your aunt too," I said as I let out a little giggle and a big smile.

We both started laughing hard because I knew if I kept the argument up I wouldn't hear the end of it with Mercedes. That's just the way she was but I loved her for who she was.

"When the last time you been to see your old therapist," Mercedes asked me?

"Who D. Betty Love? You know she got married and moved away from here about five years ago," I replied.

"Dang, I had needed her information for a friend of mines," Mercedes replied.

"She has been MIA for a minute friend. I wish she was still around to hear all about my problems but nope, she moved," I replied.

"I'm happy someone gets their fairytale ending because your ass is twenty-six and still a virgin," Mercedes announced just as we were getting out of the cab. The cab driving starting laughing right after she said that and pulled away.

"Mercedes," I said as I slapped her on her arm hard as I could.

"Ouch, don't be hitting me because I'm telling the truth. You got to let someone pop your cherry one day," she uttered without a care in this world for my feelings.

"You can say have sex, I'm not a little girl. I do know what sex is," I announced just as Mercedes was opening the nail salon door. Every last person in the

nail salon turned in looked at me like I had said something horrible.

"Girl hush, you making everyone stare at us," Mercedes processed to say.

I looked back at the customers and the Korean's that had stopped to doing nails and toes just to look up at me to be nosy and rolled my eyes then snapped off on Mercedes with an attitude.

"You hush, you the one started this conversation," I replied rolling my eyes at her a little harder.

That's when the Korean lady asked, "You two both want full set?"

"Yea, we both are getting a full set and a pedicure to, for the both of us," Mercedes uttered back at her without acknowledging my comment back to her.

"What color you gonna get," Mercedes asked me as she picked up a black bottle of nail polish.

"I don't know maybe a sky blue since that's my favorite color," I replied.

Even though Mercedes got on my nervous I enjoyed her company. We took our set in the Korean massage chair where you got your feet did and as the massage chair started to massage me I felt like It had just taken about ten pounds off my shoulders. If you ever been in a massage chair then you know how good that shit feels. I laid my head back and just let it massage my body. I didn't know what a nut felt like but I knew I could just nut right now how good I was feeling in this massage chair.

"You ok? You over there looking like you 'bout close

to catching a nut," Mercedes said.

"Ugh, girl hush stop talking like that," I replied mean mugging her ass for interrupting my peace of mind.

"No, but for real, Da'wan and Nick as invited us out to dinner tonight if you down to go. I mean it is free food with two successful lawyers," Mercedes announce shrugging her shoulders up like she was innocent.

"Mercedes, I knew it was some reason you were beginning so nice. You were trying to butter me up for a double date," I uttered lower my eyes reading right through her bullshit.

"Bestie, just one night. For me please, I didn't want to tell Da'wan you turned down the offer so I had to do what I had to do. I haven't seen him all week he been super busy and I need this date," Mercedes utter as she pleaded for me to say, yes.

"I will do it for you this one time since I'm taking your money for this pedicure and my nails but just know you owe me big time," I announced. I hated how I loved my bestie and sometimes her ass would use it against me. I just wanted her to be happy at least one of us should have a fairytale ending and besides Da'wan was a nice handsome guy who treated her right.

Chapter 5

NICK- AFTER THE PARTY

I couldn't lie, I enjoyed seeing all of my childhood friends and my cousins that I hadn't seen in years. Bella had gotten a little tipsy and was falling all over me. She even went so far as to placing a few kisses on my cheek, but for some reason, I wasn't really into her. Since the party, Ocean was on my mind, and I was surprised that I even liked her at all. I normally didn't like nor had I ever been into women on the thicker side. Even though Bella had a small frame, I wasn't into her like I used to be when we were just kids. But I had that feeling like I knew everything about her, and it just wasn't anything new to learn. Ocean, on the other hand, was downplaying me to the left, plus I felt like it was more to her story than she was telling me.

"Can you take me home?" Bella asked in a drunken slur.

"You didn't drive?" I asked her, pulling her arm

from around my neck but still at the sametime I was trying to hold her up.

"I did, but I'm too wasted to drive," Bella replied.

"I kind of have a date, and I don't want to be late. You can't ride with neither one of your friends?" I asked her, trying to say it in a nice way. Da'wan had just texted me and told me to meet him at the restaurant at nine o'clock.

"They both left an hour ago while I was over here talking and flirting with you," Bella replied.

She was right, we had been sitting down talking about the old days, but I didn't drink anything. Bella, on the other hand, was throwing the cocktails back like it was nothing.

"Ok, where is your place located?"

"It's in Manhattan, New York."

"Wow, that's damn near an hour drive," I replied.

Before I could say anything back to her, she was about to pass out in my arms. I had my father open my car door as I placed her in my front seat.

I hated to stand Ocean up, but I couldn't just leave Bella at my father's house. Her parents had left, and so did both her friends.

It took thirty minutes to get to Manhattan which was a little more than forty-five minutes away from Brooklyn, so I had a good little drive to get Bella home. Just when I went to turn up the music, Bella woke up out of her sleep. Before she could get a word out of her mouth, all I could see was her throwing up all over herself and my passenger seat in the front of my car.

"Pull over, please," Bella requested.

"Ok, give me second," I said before I saw a clear spot to stop and pull over. Once we pulled over, I looked down at my cell phone, and Da'wan was calling yet again for the fourth time. I picked up his call.

"Hi Da'wan," I said as I picked up my cell phone.

"Where the hell is you, brah?" Da'wan asked.

"It's a long story, but just know I had to help a friend get home because she was a little too tipsy."

That's when Bella tapped me on my shoulder. "I feel much better, and I'm ready now," she said.

"Hi, man please tell Ocean I will make it up to her," I replied before I hung up the phone.

When we did get back on the road, I looked at my clock in my car on my touch screen radio, and it read ten o'clock on the dot. I had not only missed the whole dinner, but I wasn't enjoying Bella's vomiting smell coming from the passenger side to the driver side where I was.

I rolled down the window to let the air come through in hopes that it would kill the smell, but it only made it worse.

"I'm sorry about throwing up in your car," Bella said as I pulled up to her luxury condos that had a nice view of the whole New York City.

"It's no problem, I'm just happy that you're feeling better," I announced.

"Give me your number so I can pay for your car to get clean," Bella said.

"You don't have to do all that. I will get it cleaned myself like I always do."

"I insist that I do it for you," Bella replied giving me a puppy dog look.

"917-232-4414," I said without another thought. I was just ready to get back to my side of town so I could at least check up on Ocean.

"Thank you. You sure you don't want to come up? You can stay the night if you like," Bella uttered.

I couldn't believe the words that had come out of her mouth. I just had told her I had a date, and she just didn't care at all.

"Bella, you are a nice person and all, but I'm really into someone else. I was supposed to have met her tonight which she probably never wants to see me again because I just stood her up. Go ahead upstairs and get you some coffee, love."

"Goodnight Nick, please tell her I'm jealous, and that she is one lucky girl."

◦◦◦◦◦

When I did make it back to my side of town, it was a little past eleven o'clock. I figured by now, Ocean never wanted to hear my name again. Once I had pulled up to my apartment, I shot Mercedes a quick text praying that she would respond back to me.

Me: Is it anyway I could get Ocean's number?

Mercedes: Who is this? And who gave you my number?

❦ 30 ❦

Me: This Nick and Da'wan gave it to me. Is you around Ocean right now?

Mercedes: Nope, I'm sure she never wants to hear from you again.

Me: I have you five hundred dollars if you give me her number, please. I'm really sorry, I had a family emergency.

Mercedes: Cash app me my money first and then I'll give it to you.

Me: What's your Cash app name?

Mercedes: $Mercedes22

Me: Check it now, I just sent it.

Mercedes: 917-600-6201

Me: Thank you so much, I will never forget this.

Soon as I got off the phone with Mercedes I called Ocean phone but of course, nobody picked up. So I texted her to let her know it was me.

Me: Hi, Ocean this is Nick Rizzo. Please give me a call asap.

Ten minutes went by and still no reply. I still had a lot to learn about women, but I wasn't really used to having to try hard for anything in my life besides going to college. Trying to take my mother's advice from this morning, I texted her once again.

Me: I'm very sorry for standing you up. I had a family emergency.

Ocean: Look, it really doesn't matter, Nick. I was only coming out to make my bestie Mercedes happy. We had

talked about this the last time when we was at the party. I'm not your type, and you're not mine. Have a nice life.

Me: Hold Listen, I messed up my one and only chance to win you over. I don't believe that we are not each other's type. I just feel like you're scared to try something that's not so familiar to you. So am I, I'm reaching out to you just to take you to get some ice cream. It would be my pleasure to do so just to gain your forgiveness, please.

Ocean: I don't know, when are you trying to get ice cream?

Me: Now, it's still an ice cream shop open down the road from my house. I know it's late, but I just really need to see you.

Ocean: This one time, I'll say yes.

That was the good thing about New York City, there were the city that never sleeps, so just like there were people out walking in the morning, it was people out walking around late at night. There were many stores that didn't close and were open for twenty-four hours a day which was called Baskin-Robbins, this shop was nothing but six minutes away from my condo and had some of the best ice creams in all of Brooklyn. My mother used to always take me there when she wanted to apologize to me about anything when I was little, so I was using one of her techniques to see if it would work on Ocean.

Before heading to pick her up, I cleaned out the passenger seat of my car and wiped everything down with bleach wipes. I sprayed a little car freshener inside to make sure my car smelled nice for her. I just still couldn't believe Bella vomited in my car.

❧❧❧

Chapter 6

OCEAN- ICE CREAM DATE

I stood out in front of my aunty's apartment in the cold waiting to see Nick's car pull up. All I could think was this white boy better not stand me up again. I felt really stupid at the Restaurant with Mercedes and Da'wan so I just ate my food and took a cab back home. It was no way I was gonna be the third well. Soon as I looked up from wrapping my scarf tighter Nick was pulling up in a nice ass car called a Ferrari. I know Mercedes told me that Nick was a lawyer but it was no way he could afford a car like that as a new lawyer.

It was no way possible that he was making that type of money to afford that car. I didn't know what else Nick was doing on the side for a living but I assumed whatever it was he had to make a lot of money doing it. Nick got out of the car, opened my car door to let me get into the passager side of the car.

"Hi love," he said.

"Hi Nick," I replied in a dry tone. I wasn't too happy to be back outside in this cold ass weather at all.

Once he got back into the car he turned the music on and my favorite song "Unthinkable by *Alicia Keys* was playing, "This my favorite song," I announced as I started singing.

"Oh for real, then let me turn it up," Nick said.

I just started singing like I wasn't even in Nick car and it made me feel a whole lot better.

"Moment of honesty

Someones gotta take the lead tonight

Who's it gonna be?

I'm gonna sit right here

And tell you all that comes to me

If you have something to say

You should say it right now

You give me a feeling that I never felt before

And I deserve it, I think I deserve it

It's becoming something that's impossible to ignore

And I can't take it

I was wondering maybe

Could I make you my baby

If we do the unthinkable would it make us look crazy

If you ask me I'm ready

If you ask me I'm ready"

Uniquely Lashay

When I was done singing my poor little heart out Nick turned the music down and asked, "Have you ever thought about singing for a living?"

"I have some side gigs booked but that's about it. Being a professional singer is something that I can't commit to right now because I have to look after my aunt," I told him.

"Oh wow, you have an amazing voice is the only reason I asked," Nick responded.

"Yea, my father used to tell me the same thing," I replied.

"He didn't lie, you sounded amazing," Nick uttered.

"So Nick tells me who gave you my cell phone number," I asked waiting for him to say Mercedes did it. She would do some shit just like that trying to get my love life off the ground.

"Nobody to be honest. I'm a lawyer remember we good at finding out stuff," I said trying my best not to give Mercedes up.

"Ummm, I don't believe you," I uttered.

"Have you ever had ice cream at Baskin-Robbins," Nick asked me as we pulled into the parking lot of the ice cream place.

"Nope, I don't really get out much and I most definitely don't go where it is a lot of white people," I said letting it slip out of my mouth.

"What you mean by that? You don't like to be around whites," Nick asked with this concerned look upon his face.

"It's not that I don't like them I just never was to use to being around them until I move here to New York when I was about nine years old so I'm just still a little stuck in my way. No offense to you or nothing," I replied.

"No offense taken. I know how you feel. When I am around Da'wan sometimes I would be the only white or Italian guy hanging out with him but It was a little abnormal but then eventually I got used to it," Nick replied.

"I guess, you can say that. I work around whites at the hospital all day every day but it's not the same as me actually having to be around them all the time. That's just eight hours out of my day and I just try my best to stay out of there way. That's just what my father taught us to do back when I lived in Macon, Ga," I replied.

"That explains it then your not originally from New York. See most of New York people are so used to everyone being together that is no problem for us," Nick uttered.

"Yes, when I first went to school down here back in 2002 I was so shocked to see all the kids of a different color all in one class. A lot of kids used to think I acted weird but not my bestie Mercedes," I told Nick.

"You and Mercedes are pretty close. You can wait in the car while I get our Ice cream to go if you want. We can eat in right sitting in my car in the parking lot," Nick replied.

"That's so sweet of you, really it is," I uttered back.

"What is your favorite kind of ice cream," Nick

asked?

"Cookies and cream," I said.

"How do you want it on a cone are in a cup," he uttered?

"It doesn't matter surprise me," I uttered back.

I couldn't believe It I was twenty-six years old and finally out on my first real date. In the crazy thing about it that I would never have guessed my first date would be an Italian guy. Although, I would have loved a strong black male like my father. I was actually enjoying Nick's point of view and his mind frame. He had a great outlook on life and plus he understood where I was coming from with the way I was brought up. I didn't quite know his background but for what he had shown me in just this hour he seemed like someone I could vibe with.

Once he returned with my ice cream which he put on a cone-like I assumed he would do anyway, he got into the car and handed me the ice cream.

"We better eat them before they melt," Nick uttered looking at me as I took my first lick.

"Why are you watching me lick my ice cream," I asked?

"You look so cute doing it. It's just the way you are licking it," Nick replied.

"And what way is that," I uttered waiting for his answer?

"The way you are doing it. I love how you close your eyes on every lick," Nick answered without having to think about his answer.

"Hush, let me see how you look when you lick yours then," I told him.

"No, I think I might look ugly," He answered.

"Not with those honey brown eyes and that cute smile you giving me right now," I said letting it slip out before I could catch myself.

"Somebody thinks I'm handsome," Nick uttered smiling as he took another lick of his ice cream.

"Well, I kind of like the suits dress code you have to. You look like you can be a mob boss," I uttered as I giggle a little with it.

Nick must have thought what I said was funny because he giggled right along with me.

"So tell me a little more about Ms. Ocean with the short hair cut," Nick asked?

"For starters, my low hair cut means so much to me. I know a lot of people see me with my low haircut and wonder why I rock it. It's was actually the last gift I gave my mother who had went bald from chemo before she passed away with cancer," I announced as a small tear escaped my right eye. I tried to catch it but it had already rolled down my cheek before I could catch it. That's when Nick wiped my tears as they flowed down my like a river after the first tear drop, with a napkin.

"I'm so sorry I asked you about your hair. I had no idea and could never imagine losing my mother," He said in a soft tone.

" Yea, it was hard at first but now that the time has passed it's getting easier. My father passed away before my mother so you would never imagine the feeling of

losing two parents not just one. I pray and talk to them daily but that will never bring them back," I replied.

"I'm thankful you telling me your story because your not the same girl I bumped into. I promise I thought you were this mean black woman who was angry with the world. Now that I'm talking to you and I know your story it helps me understand you better," he announced.

"It's a lot of people that try to judge me but don't really get to know me but I try my best to stay to myself. For one thing, my view of the world is way different than others. The pain I had endured is way higher than any child should ever have to endure when they are just a kid," I said letting him know exactly how I felt about what I went through when I was young.

"You right I couldn't imagine but just know my life is not peaches and cream either," Nick said then bit his ice cream cone.

"What do you mean? You seem to have everything together," I uttered.

"Do I? I know it look that way but I disappoint my old man daily just by not obeying is rules or agreeing to the arranged marriage that was setup by my parents when I was just a baby. See you don't know just how much freedom you truly have. And know that I have met you I'm definitely not marrying nobody," Nick said as he blushed a little and bit his cone once again.

"Wow, an arranged marriage? I didn't even think nobody does them no more. That is such a fifty's and sixty's type of family thing to do," I announced giving him my thoughts on his situation.

"Now you see we aren't as different as you thought we were. I have my own family problems but when people see me than assume I have my whole life together and that life is so much easier for me. I just try to make the best out of my life," Nick said answering a lot of my questions about him.

I had just finished my Ice creamed, Nick and I had been up all night talking and finding out different things about each other. I was shocked to know his parents arranged him a marriage. That was a shocker but it was getting late and I was getting sleepy. I looked at my cell phone and it read at four o'clock on the dot. Yes, it was four in the morning and we were still posted up in this Baskin-Robbins parking lot running our mouths for hours. I let out a big yawned which let Nick know that the night was over with for me.

"You're getting sleepy on me beautiful," Nick asked?

"Yea, I think I'm calling it a night," I said.

As we rode to my apartment I just looked over at Nick and I noticed how convenient he was in his own skin. He was handsome and I just knew he could have any girl he wanted to I thought, *so why did he want me?*

❦

Chapter 7

NICK- COURT

Three months had gone by, and could you believe it, but Ocean and I were still going strong? I couldn't lie, although I had grown close to her and all, I still hadn't let her meet my mother nor father. I knew my mother would love whoever I loved, but my old man was something else. He was the type that wanted to run my life and his own. Ocean was too special to me to let him run her off. I never thought I would be in love with a thick plus woman and let alone a black one. They say a person's heart has nothing to do with skin color, and they were right. Ocean was the sweetest woman I had met in a long time, and she had a heart of gold. She had finally told me she was a virgin, and I still couldn't believe at twenty-six she was a virgin, wow. Just thinking about her and her soft pink lips made my dick get on hard.

I sat in the courtroom thinking about Ocean as the judge talked about Killa Joe's case when I heard the

judge say my name. "M: Rizzo, do you hear what I'm saying to you?"

"Yes, your honor?" I said, snapping back to reality.

"Joe Cassin's murder charges for the officer's in this case will stick due to the fact we have more body camera video's coming forward for evidence." I couldn't believe my ears. Everything with this case had been going fine and was on the right track, and now he going say something shit like this.

"Your honor, I never got to see a video of my client, and this is the first I have heard of this evidence. Can we reconvene tomorrow after I see the videos?" I said, trying to buy myself some time.

The judge just didn't understand how badly I needed this case to go my way. All the other charges had been dropped and thrown out but the murder charges. Big Mike never mentioned they had no video of the shit. My palms were sweating, and as I looked over at Killa Joe, I just knew he was about to call Big Mike and tell him what the judge had just called out.

"You better get me out of here and I mean scott free, or you know what Big Mike gon' do to you," Killa Joe said, making a hand gesture like a knife was cutting his throat trying to scare me up.

I was a little scared, but Big Mike had to understand if they had them murders on video, and the videos were clear enough to see Killa Joe's face. It was gonna be hard to beat these charges.

Sitting in my seat, I didn't move because of how shocked I was. I sat there in deep thought just shaking my head because I knew shit was about to get real for

me.

Leaving the courthouse, my cell phone vibrated in my pocket about three times before I took it out to see who it was. Big Mike's picture popped up on my cell phone.

"Hi, Big Mike, I was just leaving the courtroom and was about to call you with updates on Killa Joe's case."

"Oh yeah, you see Killa Joe just called me, and he said things weren't going well in court today," Big Mike said in his deep voice.

"Yeah, see, all the other charges were dropped and today's hearing was to see whether or not the judge was gonna drop the murder charges that were pending against him. The judge came with some bullshit saying some new evidence was turned in or some shit. Look, I haven't seen the new evidence, but as soon as I do, I will let you know whether the video will be able to stick or not," I said nervous as hell. I was so nervous, it was below forty degrees, snowing, and I still had sweat popping off my forehead.

I placed a call to Ocean, but I just knew she was gonna be busy at work, but for some odd reason today, I was lucky as fuck.

"Bae, how is work going?" I said upon her picking up her cell.

"It's going great, and you called me just in time. I'm headed on break now, you want to catch some lunch together if you out of court on your lunch break?" Ocean said in her cheerful voice.

"Sure, I will swing through and pick up my pumpkin face doll," I replied, not sounding like my cheerful self.

"What's wrong with you? You don't sound like yourself, Nick."

"Nothing boo, I'm just ready to see my bae, that's all."

Once I made it to Ocean's job, she was standing outside in the cold waiting on me just like it was the very first time I had picked her up.

"What have I told you, Ocean? Don't be standing outside in the cold, bae."

"Yeah, I know. I got some good news though."

"What is that?"

"My sister Blue went into labor today and had a beautiful baby girl," she replied.

"Wow, tell her and Diego I said congratulations," I said.

"I'm so excited for her and Diego. The baby is so pretty, she reminds me a lot of our mother."

"Where you want to get something to eat at?"

"Zaxby's sounds nice. My brother Shyki will be coming home in two weekends so he can come to see the baby. I would love for you to meet him when he comes down."

"Sure bae, anyone important to you is important to me. I would love to meet him. How is *Aunty Netty* doing today?"

"She actually was back to her old self today—smiling, happy to see the baby and ready to spoil her rotten," she replied.

"I'm happy to hear that for real. I really like your

aunty and all since the first day I met her. Besides threatening me about treating you good, she's nice."

Pulling up in Zaxby's parking lot, my cell vibrated twice when I finally pulled into Zaxby's parking lot and pulled my cell out my front pocket to read it. Bella's name popped up across the screen. I pushed ignore on it and put it back into my front pocket again.

Getting out the car, Ocean reached down to tie her shoe. I jumped right behind her in a playful motion and grabbed her waist and faked like I was humping her, but really, I was just humping the air. This was something that she would do to me all the time playing, so I had started getting her back by doing it.

"Gone now, you embarrassing me," Ocean uttered trying to pull away from me.

"Oh no, you ashamed now, but when you were doing it to me yesterday, it wasn't no problem," I said letting her go.

I placed a kiss on to her cheek just to let her know I was joking with her, and I enjoyed every minute we spent together.

Once we had made it on the inside of Zaxby's, Ocean took her seat, and I took my cell and my keys and placed them on the table and went to the counter to order our food. After ordering our food, I walked to the bathroom forgetting that I had laid my cell and keys on the table. Upon making it into the bathroom, I splashed water on my face. I tried my best to shake off the negative thoughts that were coming across my mind. The whole issue with Big Mike and Killa Joe was worrying the hell out of me. I used the bathroom, washed my hands, and headed back to pick up the food

from the front. After grabbing our food tray, I walked back towards our table. That's when I saw Ocean holding up my cell phone with Bella's number on it.

"Are you gonna tell me who this woman is that just keeps calling your phone?"

"It's not what you think, bae. Listen, I was gonna tell you about her--" I said before Ocean rudely interrupted my sentence.

"You was gonna tell me about her, really Nick? I see you have lost your mind," Ocean said, picking up her purse, getting ready to stand up.

I stood up in front of her trying to finish telling her who Bella was. "That is the number to the girl my father arranged me to marry. I don't see her like that, so you have nothing to worry about," I pleaded, trying to get her to sit back down.

"I'm sitting back down because I don't want to make a scene in these people's restaurant, but just know I don't know what to believe. The way she was blowing up your shit, it seems like you and her got more going on than just some arrangement," Ocean uttered, giving me a mean mug and an attitude like the one she had when I first bumped into her during the accident by my Condo's.

"I have no reason to lie. Have I ever lied to you in these three months we been together?"

I didn't understand why Bella would keep calling my phone when she saw I hadn't answered it the first time I sent her to voicemail. Now not only did I have the case on my mind but Ocean was mad and didn't believe me. This day couldn't get any worse for me.

Chapter 8

OCEAN- THE BABY SHOWER

Two weekends had rolled around so fast, and Blue was home with the baby. She and the baby stayed at my auntie's place most of the time since Diego had to work and Blue was scared to stay home alone without any help with her newborn baby.

"Awww, look at her. She is so pretty like her aunty," I said, looking over Blue's shoulder smiling at my first born niece. I couldn't believe it, I could actually say I was an aunt now, and I planned to be the best aunty I could be.

"What time did Shyki say he would be getting off the Greyhound bus?" Blue asked.

"I don't know, I'm 'bout to text him now and see," I said pulling out my cell phone to text our baby brother.

"He said he's about an hour away, Blue," I said after his reply back.

I walked to the back room because two full weeks had gone by, and I hadn't responded back to any of Nick's text messages or calls. I just didn't know what to say to him, and I sure didn't want him to think that I was just a pushover either. I know I remembered him saying something about the arranged marriage his father had him in but I never knew he was still keeping incontact with the woman. The way she was blowing him up they had to still be communicating on a daily basis. I didn't want to seem like the jealous girlfriend, but damn, he should have been man enough to tell her he was in a committed relationship now. I hated how the shit just blew up in my face while we was together the other day our at lunch. Then again I felt as my man he should always keep me filled in on everything and be honest with me like I am with him.

Whenever, I walked back into the living room where my *Aunty Netty* and Blue were sitting, I heard a knock on the door. I knew it was Mercedes by the way the knock was. "It's Mercedes, so I'll get it," I announced. I heard my *Aunty Netty* start laughing, and Blue followed right behind her.

"How did you know that?" *Aunt Netty* asked.

I heard her as I was opening the door, and yep, I was right, it was Mercedes just like I had said.

"Where have you been?"

"MIA, you know working and stuff mostly," Mercedes replied as we made our way to the living room where everyone was at.

"Hi everyone," Mercedes said as she turned the corner right behind me.

"Hi, Mercedes. Ocean was right, it is *you*," *Aunt Netty* announced.

"Hey," Blue said.

"*Awww*, look at the little angel," Mercedes uttered.

"Isn't she a beauty?" I asked as we both took a seat on one of the living room sofas.

"How have things been going with you and Nick?" Mercedes asked.

"Why? Did he push you to come over here?"

"No, I was just asking, but that must mean things not goin' too well," Mercedes said.

"It's nothing major but I just found out that he still keeping in touch with the girl he was arranged by his father to marry. I just don't know how to feel about seeing her calling his phone and all. The crazy thing is he told me about the arranged married when we first got close," I announced as tears ran down my face.

"*Awww*, baby girl, if a man told you about a woman, trust it's no way that he is trying to have an affair with her," *Aunt Netty* uttered before anyone else could put their two cents in.

Mercedes grabbed me by my shoulder and pulled me close to her. "I'm gon' to kill Nick. I told him not to hurt my best friend," Mercedes replied.

"I think he is innocent because me being with my man for a while now, just know a man is not about to tell on himself. I would just try to hear what he has to say because just know nobody can work out your relationship problems but you and him," Blue uttered, adding her part as well.

Come to think about it, she was right. I hated to admit it, but my big sister was right this time.

"I'm talking it over with him, but I'm not about to be nobody's fool, especially not a white boy's fool," I said, giggling afterwards, making everyone else giggle too.

"I can't believe you just said that," Mercedes uttered then giggled even harder.

"She must like something about that white boy; she been datin' him for a while now," Blue's smart mouth butt said.

Just when I got ready to defend myself, another knock came at the door. Then I heard, "I'm home!" yelled out by someone which sounded just like my baby brother. As he made his way around the corner looking tall and handsome as always, I jumped up and placed a great big hug around his neck. I was so happy to see my baby brother, and to see him in his uniform made me proud of him.

"Shyki!" I yelled as I placed a tight hug around his neck.

"Hi, everyone. I had to surprise you guys," he announced. My Aunty Netty let out a couple of tears she was so happy to see my baby brother here in person.

"Boy, you lookin' more like your father every day," she uttered giving him a tight hug.

"Hi, Blue, let a nigga see his niece," Shyki said, making his way by the sofa she was sitting in.

That's when Mercedes stood up and gave him a hug. "Wow, you finally grew some inches," she said.

"Girl, what you mean? I been grown some inches," Shyki said as he gave her a mean mug.

I was so happy to see my baby brother. It had been almost two years since he had been gone, and all we could do was talk to him over the phone.

"Let me take your bags," I said as he handed them to me.

I took them and placed them into my room. When I walked back into the living room seeing how everyone was talking with each other and laughing and cutting up, I knew right there that God still showed favor upon my life.

"I know you cooked, *Aunty Netty?*" Shyki asked.

"Boy, y'all butts big enough to get in that kitchen and cook for an old lady like myself now," *Aunt Netty* uttered as she gave him this evil look.

"Ocean, it's on you then," Shyki announced

I made something for the baby shower, but I didn't just throw down like *Aunty Netty*, but I did a little something."

That's when another knock came to the door so Diego must have finally got off of work.

Shyki opened the door and let Diego in as we women continued to talk in the living room among each other.

That's when I saw who had walked in behind Diego. It was Nick, he remembered and showed up for the baby shower after all.

"I know Diego but who is this other young gentle-

men," Shyki said in a joking manner.

"That's Nick, Ocean's boyfriend," Aunt Netty announced to Shyki.

"I know I been gone too long if Ocean has a boyfriend," Shyki said then giggled afterwards.

"Hi everyone, I'm Nick Rizzo," Nick said as he waved his hand at everyone.

"Oh, we know who you are," I heard Mercedes say with an attitude.

"Hi Mercedes," Nick said.

"Thank you to everyone who came to welcome our beautiful baby girl "Sky" into this world," Diego announced as he placed a kiss onto Blue's forehead.

I just looked at Nick and still couldn't believe he came after how mean I had been treating him. He was looking at me, and I was looking at him. Our eyes locked together, and I knew right then I truly missed him. I walked over beside him and whispered into his ear, "Can we talk for a minute?"

"Sure," he looked at me and said.

I looked Nick up and down, just to see he was fresh as fuck he had on his dark Gray Armani suit tailored to fit him perfectly and his all-white Armani shoes that matched. I could tell he had been to work because that was the only time he would wear gray was when he had court. I led Nick to my room as he followed me to the back away from everyone else.

Once we made it to the back, we entered my room. As soon as we entered the room, Nick caught me off guard and placed a passionate kiss upon my lips. He

was tonguing me down, so that let me know he had missed me these two weeks just as much as I missed him.

"Now, what were you about to say?" Nick looked me in my eyes and asked. He still had my face in between his hands as if he wanted to kiss me again. By now, he had me stuttering trying to get my words out so he would understand them.

"Well, I wanted to apologize about snapping you up at Zaxby's," I finally said.

"No, you were right. Bella didn't have any business calling me like that. You just have to understand that Bella and I have always been friends, but me as a man, I know how to control myself when it comes to breaking your heart. I wouldn't do anything to break your heart, Ocean. You just too special to me, and just know I thought about you every day we have been away from each other," Nick uttered, making me cry because I knew he really cared for me.

"I believe you, Nick, but you have to let her know I'm here to stay," I said as I placed another kiss onto his lips.

❧

Chapter 9

NICK- FLEEING

After going over the video and all the new evidence for my case, I just knew I had messed up by taking this case. The video was clear as day, and Killa Joe's whole face was noticeable. I know what you guys are thinking? Yes, what the hell am I about to do? Hell, to be honest, I don't even know. Making my way out of the meeting with the DEA, I was nervous as fuck. After trying to persuade them to drop the charges or drop some time on what they were trying to give him, the only thing they came up with was twenty and do ten up front, and that was all because I talked to them down to that. I was fucked, and I just couldn't tell Killa Joe this or Big Mike. Big Mike would have so many people searching for me, and I just couldn't put Ocean in no position like that.

I had to think of something, and I had to think of something fast. That's when it came to me, I would have to leave Brooklyn. I was gonna have to flee town

period until I came up with them thirty-thousand dollars. I had like fifteen thousand left, so that left me to come up with fifteen more thousand. My mind was racing trying to figure out what I was about to do. I couldn't ask my father for help because I didn't want him to be involved in my bullshit.

I sat inside my Ferrari brainstorming hard on what was gonna be my next move. First, I was gonna have to call Ocean and let her know everything. I hated to leave her behind, but I just couldn't put her in danger like that, not after all she had been through as a child, I just couldn't. I dialed her number and waited for her to pick up the phone.

"Hi, babe," Ocean said.

"Hi, Ocean." My voice was sad.

"Why you soundin' so sad?"

"Listen, I have gotten myself involved with the wrong people, and I have to leave Brooklyn. I have to flee now, or they will kill me," I said, trying to be as honest as possible but hoping I didn't scare her.

"What? Nick, what are you talking about? Why do you have to leave Brooklyn?"

"I have gotten involved with some really bad people, and they will kill me if I don't give them the money back, and the fucked up part about it is I spent some of the money, now I'm stuck in between a rock and a hard place."

"Nobody can't let you borrow the money?"

"The only person I know got that kind of money up front is my father, but he will not give it to me unless I

go through with his stupid marriage arrangement," Nick answered.

"Bae, have you asked Da'wan? I'm sure he will help you," Ocean said.

"Look, Da'wan is a lawyer, but he doesn't make the kind of money that I make, Ocean," I replied.

"I don't want you to leave Brooklyn, Nick. I love you," Ocean said. As soon as she said the three words that I had been waiting on for almost three months now, a tear just ran down my face.

"I love you too, Ocean," I uttered, trying to hold in my tears.

"Nick, listen to me. You don't have to leave. You just need to beat them at their own game."

"What do you mean?"

"Come pick me up from the house, I'm off of work today."

⁂

On my way to Ocean's house, my cell rung. I looked at my touch screen in my car, and Da'wan's name flashed across the screen.

"What's good?" I said as I answered the phone.

"Man, I just saw the news, and they were talking about the sentence they just gave Killa Joe," Da'wan announced.

"What? Nooooo, tell me that shit didn't just come across

the news?" I knew for a fact I was dead as fuck.

"What happened? I thought they dropped his charges?"

"Listen Da'wan, they dropped them all expect the murder charges, and the last time we went back to court, they found new evidence to make the murder charges stick. After looking at the videos and evidence they had, there was no way I could persuade them to let him out even on good behavior. Man, I'm fucked!" I said.

"Wow, damn, I didn't know all this shit happened. So, what the hell are you gonna do?"

"I don't know. I took the thirty-thousand dollars, and I only have fifteen-thousand left out of the thirty-thousand, so you tell me what is about to happen?" I responded to Da'wan.

"Listen to me. I might know someone who can let you hold that kind of money. I'll call you back in an hour, but until then, just lay low."

Just as I was getting off the phone with Da'wan and pulling up to Ocean's apartment, Big Mike's name flashed across my screen. My phone rung two times before I picked it up.

"Big Mike, I was just about to call you," I said.

"Oh, you were? I just saw the news about the case, so just know you have forty-eight hours to give me the whole thirty-thousand back. You already know what's gonna happen if you don't," he said before hanging up the phone.

Just as he hung up the phone, Ocean came out of the apartment. She was looking all beautiful and cute. I just hated that any of this happened.

"Hi babe," Ocean said as she entered the car.

"Ocean, I'm about to have to flee. Big Mike, the dude I got mixed up with, is a blood. He's head over the gang, and if I don't have this man's money, there is no telling what he might try to do."

"Nick, it's ok. Listen to me, you don't have to flee nowhere, you just have to beat him at his own game. Listen, I want you to call and arrange a meeting with him in a public place, right? I want you to place a small recorder into the front pocket of your jacket, and I want you to hand him the bag. While you doin' all this, I'm somewhere sitting in your parked car calling the police. As soon as they arrive, I'ma give you a signal. You run as soon as you hand him the bag; I want you to run as fast as you can towards the car," Ocean stated.

"I don't know, Ocean."

I was nervous as fuck and didn't know what I should be doing. I needed to go to the house and get my Glock 43 .9mm. I didn't feel safe out in the streets right now.

"I need to go to my condo and get something," I said.

"Look, I know you're book smart, but I'm street smart, and going back to your condo is not safe at all. Where do you think gon' be the first place they look?" Ocean asked me.

"You right, but I need the gun to even set up any meeting."

"Ok, we gon' just go over there and pick up the gun then leave. We cannot be there longer than five minutes," Ocean said.

I didn't know what Ocean knew about this type of

stuff, but she made some good points. I called Big Mike and sat up the meeting as Ocean told me to. I told him to meet me at the Brooklyn Botanic Garden park which was only eight minutes away or right down the road from my condo.

＊

Chapter 10

NICK-CAUGHT UP

I grabbed my Glock from my condo and put on a more comfortable suit which was all white. Once I made it back outside to my car where Ocean was sitting waiting on my return, I opened the back door, threw the bag in the back seat, and got into the driver's seat. I had my shades on, and I could feel Ocean eyeballing me down.

"What?" I said.

"I told you five minutes. That means you didn't have time to change clothes like you're going to a fashion show," Ocean said.

"It only took five minutes."

"More like eight and a half," Ocean uttered back.

"Us men don't take all day to get dressed like you women," I stated.

"You might have a valid point there," Ocean said.

"We gon' head to Da'wan's spot until eight o'clock," I said because I didn't want to be driving around; they could be following us.

"Ok, let me text Mercedes and see if she can meet me over there. I don't want to be the only girl there with just the guys," Ocean responded.

"What's wrong with us guys?" I replied.

"Nothing, I just texted Mercedes, and she is on her way."

Pulling up to Da'wan's new place, I looked around before getting out the car just to make sure we hadn't been followed or anything.

"It's clear," I announced to Ocean so she could get out of the car.

"Ok, thanks," Ocean replied as she stepped out of the car.

As soon as we walked up, Da'wan opened the door not giving us time to even ring his doorbell.

"Come on in, man," Da'wan said.

"Hi, Da'wan," Ocean uttered.

"What's good, Ocean," Da'wan responded.

"Man, you done got yourself into some Denzel Washington type of stuff," Da'wan said as he looked at me.

"I know this shit is getting crazy. I'm nervous as shit. Ocean actually came up with a great idea though, so I just arranged this meeting with Big-Mike. I just hope the shit works for real, I just want my life back," I responded.

"What is you about to do? I called that dude, but he said he only had about five-thousand on him now," Da'wan uttered.

"I'm not gonna use no money. We just gon' use a bag full of clothes and hope the law come up just in time so I can get away without anybody getting hurt or me having to hurt anybody."

"I hope you not goin' to that meeting without being strapped," Da'wan advised.

"Oh yeah, you know I'm taking my Glock now. I'm not that dumb."

Just as I said that, Da'wan's doorbell rung. Ocean rushed towards the door before I stopped her.

"Let me see who it is," I said. I was nervous as fuck.

I walked to the door praying that it was Big-Mike in she guys following me. As I opened the door I held out my Glock pointing at the door. Once the door was opened It was only Mercedes on the other side of it.

"What is wrong with you? Why are you pulling a gun on me?" Mercedes uttered with an attitude.

"My bad, Mercedes. It's a lot going on, but Ocean will fill you in I'm sure," I said as I walked away from the door.

"Mercedes, I sure am happy to see you!" Ocean uttered.

I walked back towards where Da'wan was standing nervous as fuck.

"Ma,n you gotta stop pulling that gun unless you're gonna use it," Da'wan said.

Uniquely Lashay

"I know, you're right. I'm just scared as shit."

Eight a clock had rolled around quickly, and I nearly was about to shit in my pants thinking about having to go up against one of the biggest gangsters in the city. Da'wan and Mercedes had decided they wanted to tag along on the trip to see that Ocean and I were safe. Da'wan brought his Glock 43 as well, so now we had two guns. We sat in the car some ducked off on the other side of the street parked where we couldn't be noticed. It was a good thing my car had dark tinted windows so nobody could see us.

As I saw Big-Mike standing in the park by himself, I couldn't believe it. He actually came along like I had instructed him to. I guess he figured little old me, he could take me by himself.

"Watch your surroundings, it might look as if he came alone, but trust, his goons could be somewhere hiding just like we are," Ocean said as she placed a kiss upon my lips.

As I got out of the car, I saw Ocean picked up the phone and dialed 911 so everything was full in action, and all I had to do was stick to the script.

I walked up to the park slowly giving the cops enough time to be on their way.

I walked up to Big-Mike scared out of my mind, but I wasn't about to let him know that.

"I just want to give you your money and move on

with my life," I said as I approached him. I had the recorder in my front pocket running the whole time.

"This is not just about the money. Did you know Killa Joe is my big brother? He can't do no ten years in prison, so someone gotta pay," Big-Mike said.

"What do you mean someone gotta pay? I did everything I could for Killa Joe's case just like I would for any other case I did for you in the past. I didn't want things to go down like this," I uttered.

"I don't believe they had a video on my brother. I believe you workin' the state to pin some shit on my brother," Big Mike uttered, and right when he said that, he tried to rush me, but I jumped back and dropped the bag. I ran through a crowd of people, so I couldn't pull out my gun because I didn't want to shoot not innocent people.

As I ran through the crowd, I made it by a big tree that I ran behind. I could hear him huffing and puffing looking for me. I pulled out my cell phone and called Ocean.

"Is the cops here yet?" I asked as she picked up the phone.

"Yes, they're coming into the park now. Run towards them!" Ocean screamed. I saw one cop approaching me, and I took off running as fast as I could.

As I ran towards the cops, Big-Mike spotted me and started running quickly after me. Before I could make it to the cop, he shot me in my leg.

I went tumbling down to the ground, and all I could hear was the cops yelling, "Man down." That's when I heard them take about ten more shots, and Big-Mike

fell to the ground making a loud scream from the pain of the ten shots they had given him before he made it to me to shoot me again.

I looked up to the sky to see nothing but stars shining in my face then an Angel appeared to me.

"You will be ok. You did great, now it's all over," Ocean said.

"Brah, I'm happy he didn't shoot you in your back or nowhere," Da'wan said standing next to her.

"He should have killed your ass for pulling that gun on me earlier!" Mercedes uttered.

My leg was hurting, but I was so happy that it was over so now I could live the life I wanted to with my soon to be wife, Ocean. Yeah, you heard me, I'm popping that question as soon as my leg heals up, and I'm back on my feet.

Chapter 11

OCEAN- THE BIG QUESTION

Six Months Later...

Nick's leg had healed up nicely, and he was back walking again. Mercedes and Da'wan were happy and still dating. Blue and Diego had their wedding about four months ago. Yes, I was her maid of honor. See, after the passing of my mother, Blue and I actually became a lot closer. Sky, Blue, and Diego's daughter was getting bigger and looking more and more like my mother as each day passed. My mental health was still under control, so your girl could handle anything that came my way.

I have moved in with the love of my life and he wasn't taking any more money on the side of his regular clients as I had instructed him. I was actually in a good space and happy again. I had finally met Nick's mother, and we actually were getting along great. After everything that happened in my life, I was in a

good space. Last but not least, I was no longer a virgin anymore. I lost my virginity at the age of twenty-seven, but it was so worth the wait.

I was still working at the hospital, I had even got promoted and a fat ass raise. Big-Mike ended up living even though he got shot ten times, but he was now serving time with his brother for Attempted Murder for trying to murder Nick.

I just got home to our new condo that Nick and I had just moved into. It had a perfect view of the whole New York city, and I would stand out on the top of the buildings some nights and just release how thankful I was that I came to this city at the age of nine. I would have never met my soul mate, Nick, even though he was white/Italian, and I'm black, we both had good hearts, and that was all that mattered.

I called for my man upon entering our new home.

"Nick, where are you?" I screamed.

"I'm in here!" Nick screamed back.

When I entered our bedroom, Nick was naked with rose petals all over the bed with a ring in his mouth.

I walked closer to the bed and snatched the ring out of his mouth. It was a 14K White Gold Inside Round Solitaire Engagement Ring. It was beautiful and was the one that I had pointed out to him about a month back.

"Awww, Nick," I said as I looked at my ring.

"Ocean Ray, will you do me the honor of being Mrs Rizzo?"

"I will, I do, yes, I will marry you."

The End!!!

What Makes You Unique:

Reaching for your goals no matter who doubts you is what makes you unique. Not letting this world take your creativity and remaining humble no matter what causes you to stand out. When life gets tough, don't give up, just keep pushing for the stars. The people that shine the brightest are often the ones who have been down the darkest roads.

About Author

Lashay Perkins, pen name is Uniquely Lashay, has a degree in Health Care Administration, works full time in the medical field, and she is a part- time writer. She wants to further her future in writing full time. She is a mother of three kids and two dogs; one is named King, and the other one is named Prince. She loves to write in her free time. She lives in Bainbridge, Ga but has also resided in Jacksonville, Fl for the past ten years. Writing and reading have always been a joy for her since she was a child. She enjoys telling stories for the curvy women around the world. It has always been her pleasure to share her view on the world. Writing has always helped her to escape from her everyday reality. She hopes her work is enjoyable and entertaining.

Uniquely Lashay

Keep In Touch with Uniquely Lashay

Facebook: @Uniquely Lashay

https://www.facebook.com/profile.php?id=100027014030850

Instagram: @fancyshay1

https://www.instagram.com/fancyshay1/

Twitter: @fancyshay

https://twitter.com/fancyshay1

Wattpad: @fancyshay1

https://www.wattpad.com/user/fancyshay

Author Page: @AuthoressUniquelyLashay

https://www.facebook.com/AuthoressUniquelyLashay/

(Facebook) Promotion page: @Unique Creations book Promotions

https://www.facebook.com/groups/2028167847297707/

Interview By OG Publications

http://www.ogpublications.com/interrogation-room-meet-author-lashay/

Interview By Voyage Magazine

http://voyageatl.com/interview/meet-lashay-perkins-uniquely-lashay-currently-live-bainbridge-ga/?fbclid=IwARirQqNxTJFTVGMyfmwpJZJC7Awe-WmX-RiLkaXWUYkmycfWDtB-VxgnUyaI

Uniquely Lashay

Looking for a Publishing home? Hit us up if you are looking for a family, not just a business. Let us show you the real meaning of publishing with love, respect, and hard-work. We accept experienced and aspiring writers. We will give the aspiring writers guidance and mentoring to make it in this industry. (Unique Creations Publications) is now accepting submissions in all genres.

uniquecreationpublication@gmail.com

The Things We Never Say 2

Now Available

Coming May 25th

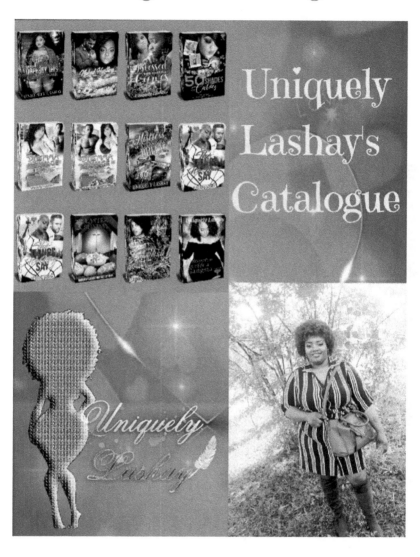

Uniquely Lashay's Catalogue

Now Available on Amazon
@ amazon.com/author/uniquely

CPSIA information can be obtained
at www.ICGtesting.com
Printed in the USA
LVHW021750270619
622554LV00016B/948

Unique Creations Publications is now accepting
manuscripts from aspiring & experienced authors!

The Things We Never Say 2

A Novel By

Uniquely Lashay